to preface:

this book is for mature audiences only. you'll probably be asking yourself why you bought this book when you're done reading it. that's the whole point.

kisses xoxo mwah <3

table of contents

o vaginitis vaginitis
please go away
you know i can't fight this
your presence in my pussy
really fucking puts me
on edge every day
because i can't queef
it hurts too much
this pain i'm feeling
makes my pussy so dry
that it's cracking and peeling

~ *what ophelia felt whenever she looked at hamlet after he started acting crazy*

you were my first love
you were my first time
i would never leave you
especially since you gave me chlamydia

he accidentally pissed himself
in the middle of making out
he was embarrassed
but i was turned on
so i pissed myself too

she squeezed and squeezed
and one at a time
popped out
an anal bead

she never knew how
or when
or why
but whencver she saw him
she always
queefed

her lips tasted like cranberries
and her kisses were sweet
but he was blind
because he was actually
raw dogging plain meat

the women cried in agony that night
once they realized
they couldn't scissor each other
because their clits were too big

her clitoris stretched far and wide
so she wrapped it around his neck
and took him
for a ride

the first time we met
you sharted
and i thought to myself
should i do it too?

pussy pussy pussy pussy pussy pussy pussy
pussy pussy pussy pussy pussy pussy pussy
pussy pussy pussy pussy pussy pussy pussy
pussy pussy pussy pussy pussy pussy pussy
pussy pussy pussy pussy pussy pussy pussy
pussy pussy pussy pussy pussy pussy pussy
pussy pussy pussy pussy pussy pussy pussy
pussy pussy pussy pussy pussy pussy pussy
pussy pussy pussy pussy pussy pussy pussy
pussy pussy pussy pussy pussy pussy pussy
pussy pussy pussy pussy pussy pussy pussy
pussy pussy pussy pussy pussy pussy pussy
pussy pussy pussy pussy pussy pussy pussy
pussy pussy pussy pussy pussy pussy pussy
pussy pussy pussy pussy pussy pussy pussy
pussy pussy pussy pussy pussy pussy pussy
pussy pussy pussy pussy pussy pussy pussy
pussy pussy pussy pussy pussy pussy pussy
pussy pussy pussy pussy pussy pussy pussy
pussy pussy pussy pussy pussy pussy pussy
pussy pussy pussy pussy pussy pussy pussy
pussy pussy pussy pussy pussy pussy pussy
pussy pussy pussy pussy pussy pussy pussy

the girl had a red vajiji
the boy had blue balls
together they made
the purple nurple

he didn't always like anal
but ever since the party
ever since the night she pegged him
he realized love
knows no bounds

she poured out her love for him
and in return
he pissed into her mouth

he bought her tulips
but what she really wanted
was his two lips
to wrap around her
two clits

he looked into her eyes
and the next thing you know
they were in the backseat of the car
sharting side by side

sniff my fart
taste my shart
my pussy is ugly
don't play with my heart

she told me she liked doggy style
so i bought her a dog, dressed in style
but when i let it out during sex
it penetrated her box
and she cried for a while

live, love, laugh?
more like,
squirt,
queef,
up and down the shaft

we live in a society
where two men
can't love each other
and eat Taco Bell
at the same time

they call her the werewolf
because in the dead of night
her neatly trimmed vajookie
transforms into an untamed forest
and that's
where she keeps her secrets

he had one shaft
and two balls
it was perfect
he could stick
one in the front
and two in the nostrils

dick dick dick dick dick dick dick dick dick dick
dick dick dick dick dick dick dick dick dick dick
dick dick dick dick dick dick dick dick dick dick
dick dick dick dick dick dick dick dick dick dick
dick dick dick dick dick dick dick dick dick dick
dick dick dick dick dick dick dick dick dick dick
dick dick dick dick dick dick dick dick dick dick
dick dick dick dick dick dick dick dick dick dick
dick dick dick dick dick dick dick dick dick dick
dick dick dick dick dick dick dick dick dick dick
dick dick dick dick dick dick dick dick dick dick
dick dick dick dick dick dick dick dick dick dick
dick dick dick dick dick dick dick dick dick dick
dick dick dick dick dick dick dick dick dick dick
dick dick dick dick dick dick dick dick dick dick
dick dick dick dick dick dick dick dick dick dick
dick dick dick dick dick dick dick dick dick dick
dick dick dick dick dick dick dick dick dick dick
dick dick dick dick dick dick dick dick dick dick
dick dick dick dick dick dick dick dick dick dick
dick dick dick dick dick dick dick dick dick dick
dick dick dick dick dick dick dick dick dick dick
dick dick dick dick dick dick dick dick dick dick

tears of blood
streamed out of her vajay
she wasn't crying
she was okay
she cupped the blood
into her hands
and fed it to her boyfriend,
The Vampire Man

it took her two guys
and three tries
to realize
a six-inch dildo
was only
worth her time

you left me wondering who i was that day
why did you do that to me?
why did you shove
a tentacle up my ass?

a gleaming grin took over your face
you were happy
and so was i
because my cooter
squirted into your eye

i miss you
it’s not the same since you left me
now i have no one
to pee on the toilet with

you rode my cooter like a scooter
but you gave me anal
like an angel

i let you hold my hand
but you never let me hold your nutsack

he popped a glizzy
into her beef curtains
and together
they made
a nasty midnight stew

you ripped out my heart
so i
ripped off your clitoris

her pussy tasted like medium rare
his dick tasted like mushroom soup
together they were the perfect meal

she used to love him
harder than rain hitting
the window
harder than his semen hitting
his cum rag

you kissed me
said you loved me
then cheated on me
so what did i do?
i farted in your mouth while you were sleeping

i never once imagined that you and i
would be sitting together side by side
queefing together
from time to time

it hurt knowing that you kissed her and not me
but that’s okay
because i took a big shart in your bed anyway

forget about me
you said you loved me
but all you gave me
was anal

you said love wasn't real
you were right
now hand me my vibrator

can you hear it?
that sweet sound?
it was your pussy
that made me frown

BIG TIDDIES

Medium Tiddies

little tiddies

you ate my ass
and i ate your pussy
two tongues
intertwined
our holes ferment
to make bitter wine

you mooned me
so i shoved my foot
up your ass

i gave you head
you left me on read
until that day
you texted me again
i came over
i cut off your sack
and left you
in zen

i wanted you to want me
but i wasn't that type of girl
to tell you directly
so i left you my tampon
behind your backyard pine tree

your sack was too big
your dick was too small
you were uncircumcised
all i tasted was cheese balls

i promise you, i’ll never leave.
but please never stop
playing with my coochie

and then there were two
it wasn't me
it wasn't you
but your big
flabby pussy lips
that i thought
were pretty cool

you called my pussy fascist,
and you were right
this was the fascist pussy on the planet

vroom vroom

it doesn’t matter who you were then
as long as i can smell
your beautiful pussy farts
i’ll always be your friend

two lovers
two men
two swords
but one
had to put it
in the other's end

i cupped my hands
around your dick
but once i felt the size
it felt too ick
13 inches
is too big
my glizzy hole
will feel like a pig

my heart doesn't belong to you
my throbbing pussy does though

1 inch
2 inch
3 inch
4

your dick is so small,
yet you call me a whore?

A B C D E F G, you're such a little
bitch why'd you cheat on me?

Q R S T U V, fuck off you cunt
and fuck your mommy

now i've sang my ABC's
i hope you know
i fucked your daddy

boys be like
2 in the pink
1 in the stink

girls be like
lemme put on my strap
i'll shove it up your shaft

twinkle twinkle little star
you're the fifth person i gave mono so far

you never understood me
and that wasn't okay
you've known me for so long now
i told you i had three clitorises
days before yesterday

queef queef queef queef queef queef queef queef
queef queef queef queef queef queef queef queef
queef queef queef queef queef queef queef queef
queef queef queef queef queef queef queef queef
queef queef queef queef queef queef queef queef
queef queef queef queef queef queef queef queef
queef queef queef queef queef queef queef queef
queef queef queef queef queef queef queef queef
queef queef queef queef queef queef queef queef
queef queef queef queef queef queef queef queef
queef queef queef queef queef queef queef queef
queef queef queef queef queef queef queef queef
queef queef queef queef queef queef queef queef
queef queef queef queef queef queef queef queef
queef queef queef queef queef queef queef queef
queef queef queef queef queef queef queef queef
queef queef queef queef queef queef queef queef
queef queef queef queef queef queef queef queef
queef queef queef queef queef queef queef queef
queef queef queef queef queef queef queef queef
queef queef queef queef queef queef queef queef
queef queef queef queef queef queef queef queef
queef queef queef queef queef queef queef queef

you wore your hands around my neck
like my mother's pearls around hers
you drove me crazy
so i drove your car
the same way
i rode your dick
i crashed it
into a ditch

one big
one small
but they're both
really hairy balls

you want my pussy to glisten?
then shut the fuck up and listen

35 ways to say vagina

The Nutorious V.A.G., vagine, coochie, lady bits, poon, punani, vajayjay, cooter cooch, penis fly trap, snatch, hot pocket, vertical smile, pink taco, love tunnel, pink portal, coochie pop, eve's tunnel, lady jane, flap dragon, butter boat, the batcave, flaming lips, puff pillow, egg crate, pecan pattie, frothy creek, velvet glove, silk igloo, sticky bun, pearl hotel, magic crepe, pink mink, pussy, The Field of Dreams, woo-woo

Why do men?
Why do men?
Why do men?
Why do men?
Why do men?
Why do men?
Why do men?
Why do men?
Why do men?
Why do men?
Why do men?
Why do men?
Why do men?

FUCK MEN
FUCK MEN
FUCK MEN
FUCK MEN
FUCK MEN
FUCK MEN
FUCK MEN
FUCK MEN
FUCK MEN
FUCK MEN
FUCK MEN
FUCK MEN

you made my pussy stanky
so this fishy can't hanky panky
because you got an STD
by fuckin' all your homies

did you actually love me?
or
did you just want this punani?

shitoris clitoris
you stupid ass bitch
i just pinched off my pussy
because of your insolence

they always ask "what's the meaning of life?"
but never "girl, why is your pussy so strife?"

you said "let's fuck"
like boy you need to wait.
until I get a tummy tuck.

clit clat clut
i hate my vag but
on sunny days
my world fades
when i get a blood clot

crooked smiles and soft kisses
this fat pussy always misses
when playing catch
with big fat dick
but gobbles your balls
and turns it into
a crusty sandwich

i let you suck
on my toes
despite the fact
you had other hoes

holy shit
my pussy is hairy
but i'll still rock your shit
like a mother fucking fairy

ew. don't touch me.
you want me to turn around so you can
fuck me?
boy, chill out
i put a pussy pocket in your shoe
go fuck something else

you act like your balls are steel
but when i pull my pussy out
you are scared to feel
i thought "are you gay?"
later i found out you were into horses
but hay

you shlobbed on my knob
like corn on the cob
you spitted on it
kissed on it
but you still didn't do the job

dildos and dicks won't do the trick
i just want to rub
my big fat clit

underneath all that skin
was the head of a cherry
so red and so thin
i popped it out
and out fell cheese
i screamed in agony
get it away from me
please

you chose me, over her?
dude she's like 43
her vag is dry and hairy and musty
i hope you get herpes, fucking crusty

D

D D

D D

D D

D D

D D

D D

D D

D D

D D

D D

D D

D D

D D

D D

D D

D D D D D D

D D

D

D

D

D

D

D D

D D

D D D D

D D D D

tuna
fish
maybe cod
my pussy doesn't smell like either
it smells like frog

a hose connected to a head
this shower will put me to bed
i'll shove it on my vagina
this water flow will rock me
from cali to china

stop calling me a whore
my pussy is commie
you fucking chore

you don't understand
boys only want me
for my big juicy nipple
but i have arthritis
i'm actually a cripple

how many times
do i have to tell you
i have teeth in my vag
you can only kiss my
mouth fool

all i wanted was your love
your sensation
to pull me though
this hell that itches
my vag is infected with crabs
because you fucked other bitches

caramel
drizzled
down
my
camel
toe
my
coochie
popped
at
the
boys
below

pop rocks up my ass
turn up the bass boy
don't give me sass

ugh my vag ugh my vag ugh my
vag ugh my vag ugh my vag ugh
my vag ugh my vag ugh my vag
ugh my vag ugh my vag ugh my
vag ugh my vag ugh my vag ugh
my vag ugh my vag ugh my vag
ugh my vag ugh my vag ugh my
vag ugh my vag ugh my vag ugh
my vag ugh my vag ugh my vag
ugh my vag ugh my vag ugh my
vag ugh my vag ugh my vag ugh
my vag ugh my vag ugh my vag
ugh my vag ugh my vag ugh my
vag ugh my vag ugh my vag ugh
my vag ugh my vag ugh my vag
ugh my vag ugh my vag ugh my

what does it mean
to have a badonkadonk
so firm
and so clean
when the only ones that
look at it are ugly boys
who can't make me cream

gobble gobble
munch munch
i'll eat your dick up
like it's brunch brunch

if you want a clean kitty
don't play with boys
that'll be a pity
instead go outside
and ride a bike
take that pussy for a hike

sweet summer clementine
your vag smells like the beach
oh won't you be mine?
this pussy cannot be purchased
on Amazon Prime

tickle my cooter
tickle it pink
tickle my vag
until you can drink
all of my discharge
from the sink
until i squirt so far
that i could die
i'll turn this pussy into pecan pie

left to right
you slapped your dick
in my face tonight
my tits were oozing
and on the floor
i was done over easy
i picked my eggs back up
i was your
sausage whore

blueberries for breakfast
waffles for dinner
blueberry waffles for breakfast, lunch, and dinner

don't you hate
don't be late
girl i need this pussy ate
it's 5 past noon
it's not to soon
my tits are big
bigger than the moon

pussy queef
pussy fart
pussy likes to pee and shart

i'm glad i left you
your horse cock never satisfied me tbh

flick the bean
touch no peen
boys are gross
my pussy's green

put it up
put it in
put it down
let it spin
spin that dick
till i fly
like the dust
in the wind

you love me
you love me not
let me spit on your dick
and i'll let you touch my glock

you can
smell this pussy
lick this pussy
eat this pussy
squeeze this pussy
but never will i ever let you
pee on this pussy

"would you rather have a gay son or a thot daughter?"

boy i would rather have my pussy opened
by your cracked father

i thought you loved me back
but all you loved
was my pussy crack

you gave me everything
and i queefed it all out

oh you want my number?
you're going to have to open that ass
and shove in a cucumber

suck on my titties
suck on my clit
bitch i can't feel your
little dick

hahaha it's page
69

the day you cheated on me
was the same day i bleached my asshole

juicy pussy
loosy pussy
silly little
goosy pussy

musty dick
crusty dick
overgrown
mushroom dick

i thought you loved me
but every time you nutted in me
it was really just pee

the juiciness of my bussy
makes it feel like real pussy

vagina fart vagina fart vagina fart vagina fart
vagina fart vagina fart vagina fart vagina fart
vagina fart vagina fart vagina fart vagina fart
vagina fart vagina fart vagina fart vagina fart
vagina fart vagina fart vagina fart vagina fart
vagina fart vagina fart vagina fart vagina fart
vagina fart vagina fart vagina fart vagina fart
vagina fart vagina fart vagina fart vagina fart
vagina fart vagina fart vagina fart vagina fart
vagina fart vagina fart vagina fart vagina fart
vagina fart vagina fart vagina fart vagina fart
vagina fart vagina fart vagina fart vagina fart
vagina fart vagina fart vagina fart vagina fart
vagina fart vagina fart vagina fart vagina fart
vagina fart vagina fart vagina fart vagina fart
vagina fart vagina fart vagina fart vagina fart
vagina fart vagina fart vagina fart vagina fart
vagina fart vagina fart vagina fart vagina fart
vagina fart vagina fart vagina fart vagina fart
vagina fart vagina fart vagina fart vagina fart
vagina fart vagina fart vagina fart vagina fart

my lips are loose
i could tie a noose
around your neck
you'd call it abuse
but i won't let go
till you suck out my
pussy juice

you like my feet, they're pretty and thin
small enough to fit inside your chunky
foreskin

you sharted on me
so i queefed on you
i covered your mouth
until your feet
turned blue

piss on my mouth
piss on my tiddies
piss on my hairy asshole
don't miss your shot with my kitty

i love you on days when your pussy mad
i love you on days when your pussy is sad
even on days when i can't see your pussy
i'll still love you because your pussy is rad

the sharts of his asshole
were neon red
and the queefs of her pussy
were waffle blue
together they made
lilac gas

vaginas are gross
men are the most
please just let me butter
my mother fucking toast

oh mother of mary
why can't i carry
my double D tits
like a hand
putting on mits

pussy throb
pussy sob
eat my pussy like corn on the cob

sweet silver tongued boy
talking me up
making me feel coy
i dropped my panties
actually naw
i'd rather play
with a different toy

yes i'm a whore
i mop my pussy
on the floor
when it's soaking wet
i'll give you head
underneath the blanket

i never said anal you a-hole!
now my asshole is bleeding
and my pussy is screaming
now i'll need some healing in my soul

pussy ambiguous it needs a jury
this court hearing needs to speed up
it needs to hurry
pussy on xanax her memory's blury
damn this pussy spicy it taste like curry

love is like a vagina
you have to work to make it come
or
you have to cum to make it work

you chose me over her?
dude she's like 43
her vag is dry and hairy and musty
i hope you get herpes, fucking crusty

rock
paper
let's rub our clits and scissor
and then i'll let you
eat my chicken dinner

vagina hater
you hate my vag
because it's as big as a crater

are you male or female
it doesn't matter
as long as your healthy
as long as your pussy eats kale

we can both part ways
but my vagina farts stays
as soon as you stop eating
my gigangtic poosay

blood squirts out of my cunt
boy please don't fuck me while you grunt

hairy balls hairy balls hairy balls hairy balls
hairy balls hairy balls hairy balls hairy balls
hairy balls hairy balls hairy balls hairy balls
hairy balls hairy balls hairy balls hairy balls
hairy balls hairy balls hairy balls hairy balls
hairy balls hairy balls hairy balls hairy balls
hairy balls hairy balls hairy balls hairy balls
hairy balls hairy balls hairy balls hairy balls
hairy balls hairy balls hairy balls hairy balls
hairy balls hairy balls hairy balls hairy balls
hairy balls hairy balls hairy balls hairy balls
hairy balls hairy balls hairy balls hairy balls
hairy balls hairy balls hairy balls hairy balls
hairy balls hairy balls hairy balls hairy balls
hairy balls hairy balls hairy balls hairy balls
hairy balls hairy balls hairy balls hairy balls
hairy balls hairy balls hairy balls hairy balls
hairy balls hairy balls hairy balls hairy balls
hairy balls hairy balls hairy balls hairy balls
hairy balls hairy balls hairy balls hairy balls
hairy balls hairy balls hairy balls hairy balls
hairy balls hairy balls hairy balls hairy balls

honey on my titties yuh
honey on my titties yuh
your big fat dick gonna kill me bruh
your big fat dick gonna kill me bruh

if 1+1 is 2
and 2+2 is 4
then why isn't my pussy being fucked
like a whore?

pussy one time
pussy two time
my creamy pussy came thrice
now it's pee time

dunk that dick
into my hole
this book is so bad
but my pussy so swole

pussy lips big
pussy lips tight
pussy lips will suffocate
men that don't treat her right

i kissed you
you kissed me
this book fucking sucks
it's shitty ass poetry

wow you did it.

you made it to the end of
the world's worst poetry
book.

i hope you queefed and sharted
and maybe farted

follow my instagram @lma0poetry
to stay updated on future content <3

Printed in Poland
by Amazon Fulfillment
Poland Sp. z o.o., Wrocław

80231120R00060